A
COYOTE COLUMBUS
STORY

For Christian, Benjamin, and Elizabeth
Coyotes every one—T.K.

For Jamie, Jonathan, Stephanie and Jenessa—W.K.M.

Text copyright © 1992 by Thomas King
Illustrations copyright © 1992 by William Kent Monkman
Second printing 2002
First published in the USA in 2002

Groundwood Books / Douglas & McIntyre
720 Bathurst Street, Suite 500, Toronto, Ontario M5S 2R4

Distributed in the USA by Publishers Group West
1700 Fourth Street, Berkeley, CA 94710

We acknowledge for their financial support of our publishing program the Canada
Council for the Arts, the Ontario Arts Council and the government of Canada
through the Book Publishing Industry Development Program (BPIDP).

ONTARIO ARTS COUNCIL
CONSEIL DES ARTS DE L'ONTARIO

Canadian Cataloguing in Publication Data
King, Thomas
A Coyote Columbus story
ISBN 0-88899-155-X
1. Columbus, Christopher, ca. 1451-1506–Juvenile fiction.
Monkman, William Kent. II. Title.
PS8571.I5298C6 1992   jC813'.54   C92-093714-4
PZ7.K55Co 1992

Library of Congress Control Number: 2002110358

Printed and bound in China

A
COYOTE COLUMBUS
STORY

BY

THOMAS KING

PICTURES BY

WILLIAM KENT MONKMAN

A Groundwood Book
Douglas & McIntyre
Toronto   Vancouver   Berkeley

T WAS COYOTE who fixed up this world, you know. She is the one who did it. She made rainbows and flowers and clouds and rivers. And she made prune juice and afternoon naps and toe-nail polish and television commercials. Some of these things were pretty good, and some of these things were foolish. But what she loved to do best was to play ball.

She played ball all day and all night. She would throw the ball and she would hit the ball and she would run and catch the ball. But playing ball by herself was boring, so she sang a song and she danced a dance and she thought hard, and pretty soon along came some beavers.

Let's play ball, says Coyote.

We've got better things to do than play ball, says those beavers. We have to build a dam so we'll have a pretty pond to swim in.

That's all very nice, says Coyote, but I want to play ball.

So Coyote sang her song and she danced her dance and she thought hard, and right away along came some moose.

Let's play ball, says Coyote.

What a foolish idea, says those moose. We'd rather wade in that lovely pond over there. And they do that.

Playing ball is a lot more fun, says Coyote, but those moose don't hear her.

I better sing my song and dance my dance and think real hard again, says Coyote. And she does. And in a while, along come some turtles.

You're just in time to play ball, says Coyote.

What a sweaty idea, says those turtles. We'd much rather lie on a nice warm rock in the middle of that beautiful pond.

But who will play ball with me? cries Coyote.

Tra-la-la-la-la, sing those beavers and moose and turtles in that happy pond.

I'll get it right this time, says Coyote, and she sings her song and dances her dance and thinks so hard her nose falls off, and right away along come some human beings.

Do you want to play ball? says Coyote, and that one makes a happy mouth and wags her ears.

Sure, says those human beings. That sounds like a good idea to us.

Hooray, says Coyote, and she lets the human beings hit the ball first.

Well, Coyote and those human beings become very good friends. You sure are a good friend, says those human beings. Yes, that's true, says Coyote.

But you know, whenever Coyote and the human beings played ball, Coyote always won. She always won because she made up the rules. That sneaky one made up the rules, and she always won because she could do that.

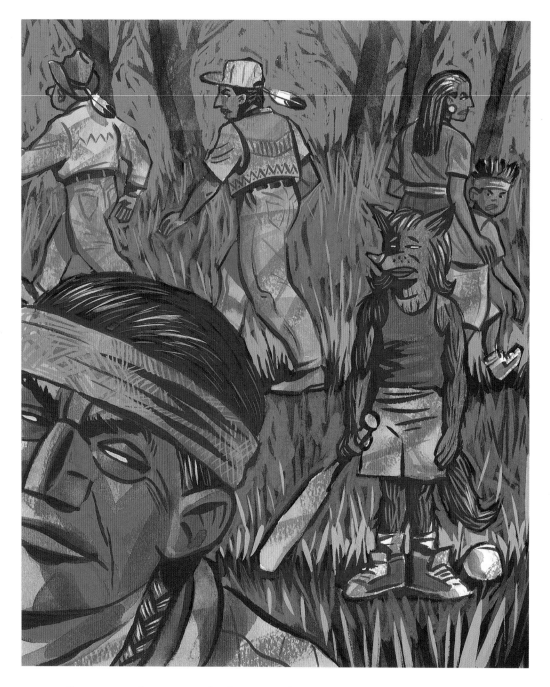

That's not fair, says the human beings. Friends don't do that.

That's the rules, says Coyote. Let's play some more. Maybe you will win next time. But they don't.

You keep changing the rules, says those human beings.

No, no, no, no, says Coyote. You are mistaken. And then she changes the rules again.

So, after a while, those human beings find better things to do.

Some of them go shopping.

Some of them go sky diving.

Some of them go to see big-time wrestling.

Some of them go on a seven-day Caribbean cruise.

Those human beings got better things to do than play ball with Coyote and those changing rules.

So, Coyote doesn't have anyone to play with again.

So, she has to play by herself.

So, she gets bored.

When Coyote gets bored, anything can happen. Stick around. Big trouble is going to come along, I can tell you that.

Well. That silly one sings a song and she dances a dance and she thinks really hard. But she's thinking about changing those rules, too, and doesn't watch what she is making up out of her head.

When Coyote stops all that singing and dancing and thinking and she looks around, she sees three ships and some people in funny-looking clothes carrying flags and boxes of junk.

Oh, happy days, says Coyote. You are just in time for the ball game.

Hello, says one of the men in silly clothes with red hair all over his head. I am Christopher Columbus. I am sailing the ocean blue looking for India. Have you seen it?

Forget India, says Coyote. Let's play ball.

It must be around here somewhere, says Christopher Columbus. I have a map.

Forget the map, says Coyote. I'll bat first and I'll tell you the rules as we go along.

But that Christopher Columbus and his friends don't want to play
ball. We got work to do, they says. We got to find India. We got to find
things we can sell.

Yes, says those Columbus people, where is that gold?

Yes, they says, where is that chocolate cake?

Yes, they says, where are those computer games?

Yes, they says, where are those music videos?

Boy, says Coyote, and that one scratches her head. I must have sung that song wrong. Maybe I didn't do the right dance. Maybe I thought too hard. These people I made have no manners. They act as if they've got no relations.

And she is right. Christopher Columbus and his friends start shouting and jumping up and down in their funny clothes.

Boy, what a bunch of noise, says Coyote. What bad manners. You guys got to stop jumping and shouting or my nose will fall off.

We got to find India, says Christopher Columbus. We got to become rich. We got to become famous. Do you think you can help us?

But all Coyote can think about is playing ball.

I'll let you bat first, says Coyote.

No time for games, says Christopher Columbus.

I'll let you make the rules, cries Coyote.

But those Columbus people don't listen. They are too busy running around looking for India. Looking for stuff they can sell. And pretty soon, they find that pond.

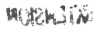

I see a four-dollar beaver, says one.

I see a fifteen-dollar moose, says another.

I see a two-dollar turtle, says a third.

Those things aren't worth poop, says Christopher Columbus. We can't sell those things in Spain. Look harder.

But all they find are beavers and moose and turtles. And when they tell Christopher Columbus, that one squeezes his ears and he chews his nose and he grinds his teeth. He grinds his teeth so hard, he gets a headache, and then he gets cranky.

And then he gets an idea.

Say, says Christopher Columbus. I'll bet this is India. And he looks at the human beings. I'll bet these are Indians. And he looks at his friends. I'll bet we can sell these Indians.

Yes, says his friends, that's a good idea. We could sell Indians. And they stop trying to catch those beavers and moose and turtles.

Whew! says those beavers and moose and turtles, that was close. And they run and hide before Columbus and his friends change their minds.

Wait a minute, says the human beings, that is not a good idea.
That is a bad idea. That is a bad idea full of bad manners.

When Coyote hears this bad idea, she starts to laugh. Who would
buy human beings, she says, and she laughs some more. She laughs
so hard she has to hold her nose on her face with both her hands.

But while that Coyote is laughing, Christopher Columbus grabs a big bunch of men and women and children and locks them up in his ships.

When Coyote stops laughing and looks around, she sees that some of the human beings are missing. Hey, she says, where are those human beings? Where are my friends?

I'm going to sell them in Spain, says Christopher Columbus. Somebody has to pay for this trip. Sailing over the ocean blue isn't cheap, you know. Grab some more Indians!

But the rest of the human beings see Columbus coming, and they jump in the pond.

I'm a beaver, they says.

I'm a moose, they says.

I'm a turtle, they says.

Hmmmm, says Columbus, and he scratches his nose. Where did all the Indians go?

They went that way says those beaver human beings and moose human beings and turtle human beings, and they point in all directions.

Wait a minute, says Coyote. What about my friends you have locked up in your ships? You got to let them go.

Tra-la-la-la-la, says Columbus, and that one goes back to Spain and sells the human beings to rich people like baseball players and dentists and babysitters and parents.

Another couple of trips like this, Columbus tells his friends, and I'll be able to buy a big bag of licorice jelly beans and a used Mercedes.

After Columbus and his friends leave, the beavers and the moose and the turtles come out of hiding, and the human beings come out of the pond.

You're supposed to fix up this world, cry those beavers and moose and turtles. You're supposed to make it right. But you keep messing it up, too.

Yes, says the human beings, you better watch out or this world is going to get bent.

Everything is okay, says Coyote. I made a little mistake but I'll take it back. I'll take Christopher Columbus back. You'll see, everything will be balanced again.

So Coyote sings her song and she dances her dance and she thinks really hard. She thinks so hard her nose falls off again, and, when she looks around, she see another bunch of funny-looking people.

Bonjour, says one of those funny-looking people. I'm Jacques Cartier, and I'm sailing the ocean blue.

I'm looking for India, says Jacques Cartier. Have you seen it?
Coyote makes a happy mouth. And that one wags her ears.
Forget India, she says. Maybe you want to play ball.

Oh, oh, says those beavers and moose and turtles and human beings. Coyote's done it again. And they catch the first train to Penticton.

Don't panic, says Coyote. Everything is under control.